L B

LITTLE, BROWN AND COMPANY
NEW YORK BOSTON

Witch Hazel

Written and illustrated by

Molly Idle

IN THE SPRING, Hilda helped Hazel sweep
the front porch.

"I've always loved this time of year," said Hazel.
"Everything old feels new again."

She brushed the hair from her forehead . . .

and the dust from the steps . . .

and smiled.

"I remember when I was your age.
My furry friend and I would spend all day
together in the sunshine, sharing stories."

"Tell me one," said Hilda.

So Hazel told one. . . .

"Tell me another!" said Hilda.

IN THE SUMMER, Hilda helped give the music room an airing.
The old piano bench creaked a bit as Hazel sat upon it.

Hazel creaked a bit, too.

She laid her hands, feather light, upon the keys.

"He and I used to make such beautiful music together.
But I loved him too much to keep him in a cage."

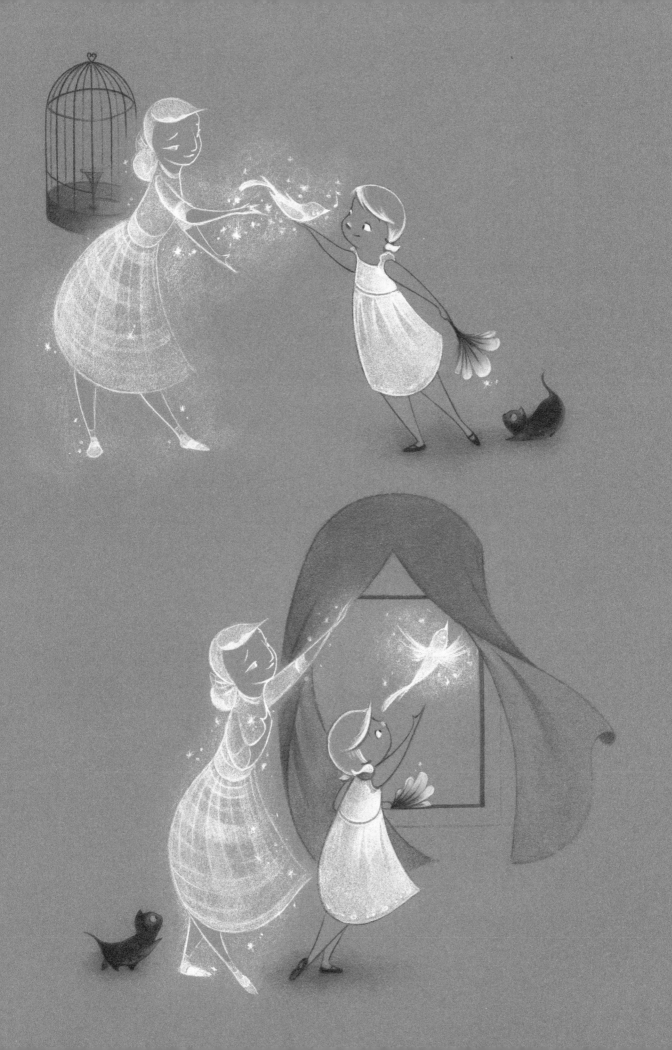

"Sometimes the warm weather makes the keys stick now," said Hazel. "Sometimes it makes me stick a bit, too. . . . I can't quite reach the high note. Can you?"

"Mm-hmm," said Hilda.

"Perfection."

In the FALL, Hilda cleared the cobwebs from the portraits in the parlor while Hazel cleared them from the corners of her mind.

"Is this you?" asked Hilda.

"Oh my, yes!" replied Hazel. "Once upon a time, I was the belle of the ball. It's a *looooong* story. . . ."

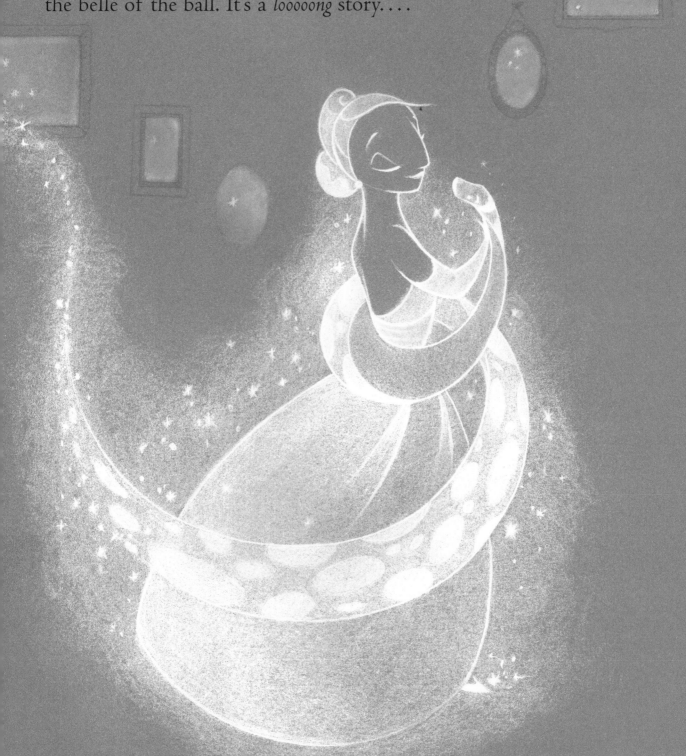

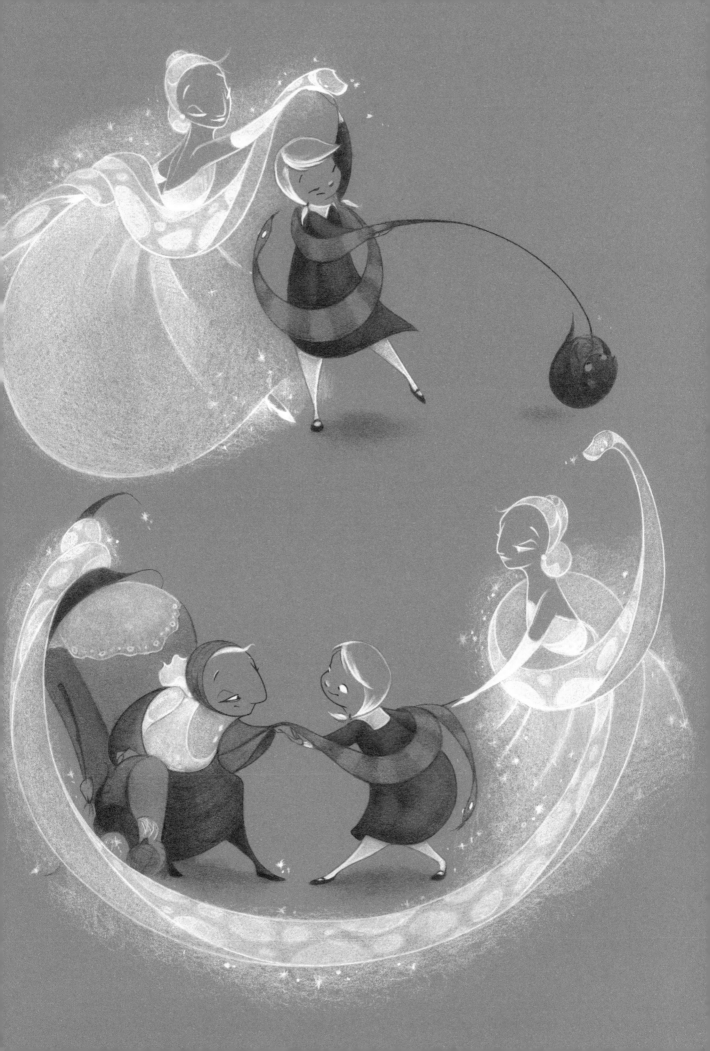

"And it was a long time ago," said Hazel.

I N THE WINTER, Hazel kept to her bed.

Hilda kept her room tidy . . .

and kept her company.

"I remember when we spent all day together in the sunshine, sharing stories," said Hilda.

"Tell me one," said Hazel.

...from the beginning...

...and another...

...and another...

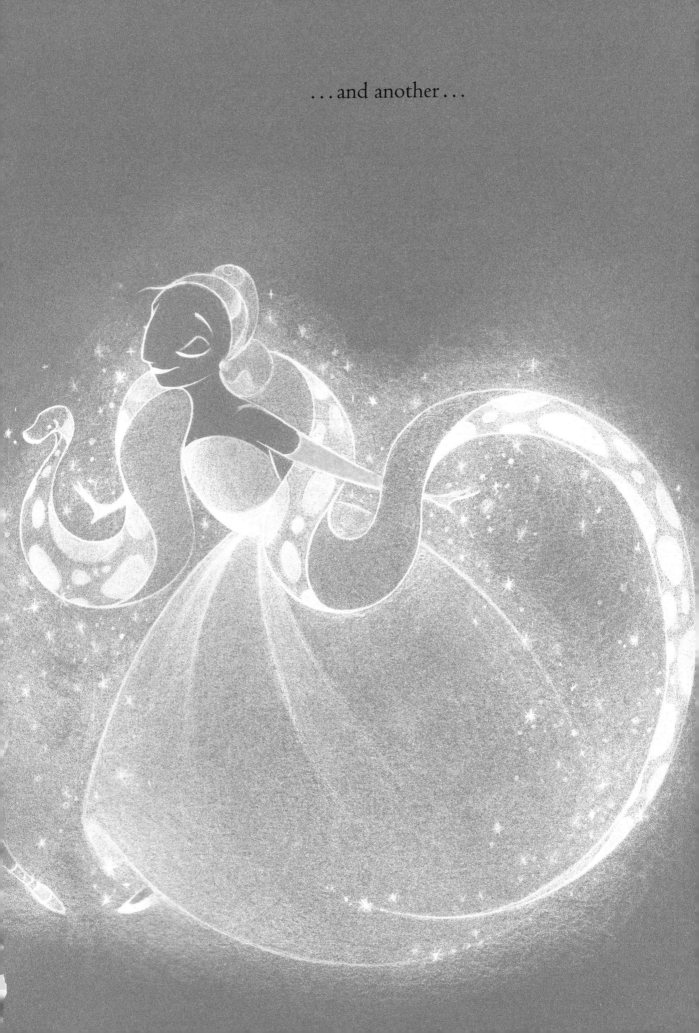

So Hilda told one . . .

. . . to the end.

IN THE SPRING, Hilda swept the front porch.

She brushed the tears from her cheeks...

and the dust from the steps...

...and smiled.

For my Manna